If We Could See the Air

written and created by
David Suzuki

art by Eugenie Fernandes

Stoddart

eugenie

To my father, Carr,
who has become
part of the wind,
the oceans, the Earth
— D.S.

First published in 1994 by
Stoddart Publishing Co. Limited
34 Lesmill Road
Toronto, Canada
M3B 2T6
(416) 445-3333

Canadian Cataloguing in Publication Data

Suzuki, David, 1936–
If we could see the air

(Nature all around series)
ISBN 0-7737-5666-3

1. Air — Juvenile literature. I. Fernandes, Eugenie.
II. Title. III. Series.

QC161.2.S89 1994   j533'.6   C94-931320-3

Editing: Jennifer Glossop
Cover Design: Brant Cowie/ArtPlus Limited

Printed in Canada on recycled paper

Stoddart Publishing gratefully acknowledges the support of the Canada Council, the Ontario Ministry of Culture, Tourism, and Recreation, Ontario Arts Council, and Ontario Publishing Centre in the development of writing and publishing in Canada.

"At last it's warm enough to go swimming," said Jamey.

His mother dipped her toe into the water. "It's still too cold for me."

"Me, too," said Megan with a shiver.

"Not for me," said Jamey. "I'm going to watch the fish."

"I'll miss all the fun," said Megan.

"We can have fun," replied Mother. "We can watch the air."

"But there's nothing there."

"Yes, there is. We can feel the air as wind and we can imagine what it looks like."

"That's neat," Megan said. "If we could see the air, would the birds be swimming in it like fish in the water?"

"That's right. The air holds the birds up. It also holds up airplanes. And it pushes sails and windmills and makes the trees bend."

"And it even steals beach umbrellas," cried Megan.

"I'm out of breath," said Megan when she got back.

"Running made your body need more air. But even when we're just sitting or sleeping, our bodies need to breathe. Without air we would die."

"Plants need air too," said Megan. "We learned all about it in school. Air is made of gases. Plants take in carbon dioxide, and they give off oxygen. Animals do the opposite — take in the oxygen and breathe out the carbon dioxide. I think it's so neat that plants and animals help each other!"

"What about fish?" asked Megan. "How can they breathe?"

"They don't breathe air," said Mother, "but they *do* need oxygen. They take it from the water. Fish breathe through their gills."

"Isn't new air being made all the time?" asked Megan.

"No, it's the same air. The gases just get rearranged. We share the air with plants and other animals. It goes out of them and into you."

"Yuk!" said Megan. "The air inside me was just inside this frog!"

"Exactly," said Mother.

"This flower smells nice," said Megan.
"That's right. Bees can smell the flowers, too.
When they come to get pollen for their honey,
they pollinate the flowers."

"Sounds are also in the air. Listen. What can you hear?" asked Mother.

"I can hear some birds and I can hear Jamey laughing. Do you hear that cricket?"

"I think so. You have good hearing, Megan. What you hear are vibrations that travel through the air like waves across the water."

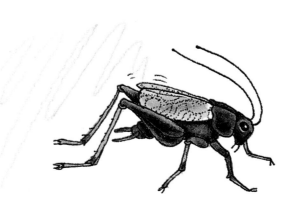

"Did you know that there's water in the air?" said Mother.

"I know — clouds. That's where rain and snow come from."

"And when it gets cold, the moisture in your breath forms a cloud."

23

"Air doesn't stay in one place," said Mother. "It goes around the world. This warm air came all the way from the tropics."

"You mean we could be breathing air from the Amazon jungle or from Africa?"

"Could be."

"Look at that! The warm air is bringing lots of clouds, too."

"Those clouds are water that rose up into the air. Maybe that water came from an ocean on the other side of the world. Up where the clouds are, strong winds always blow."

"Does the air go all the way to the moon?" asked Megan.

"No, it stays close to the earth. The farther we go from the earth, the less air there is. Way out, a layer of gas called ozone protects us from a harmful part of sunlight. Farther away still, there is no air at all."

"I guess that's why astronauts take air with them."

"Right. Without it, they couldn't breathe."

"Oh, dear, I think it's going to rain. Come on, you two. It's time to go."

"I had fun," said Jamey. "I saw a school of little fish and some ducks floating on the water."

"We saw some amazing things too," Megan told him. "We saw the air."

"No way!" said Jamey. "That's impossible."

"Not really," said Megan. "You just need imagination."

Use Your Imagination

Go back through the pages of this book. In the pictures are other things that need and use air. Can you find them? Here are some hints:

On *pages 6 and 7,* the air is flowing over and under the birds' wings. That is what holds the birds up. The hot air balloon is rising into the sky. Why doesn't it fall? Jamey is blowing air into soap bubbles, and he has filled his raft with air so it will float.

Pages 8 and 9: Unlike humans, insects don't have noses. Instead they breathe through holes in their bodies called spiracles. How do birds, mammals, and reptiles breathe?

On *pages 10 and 11* are water animals. Some, like the beaver, frog, and turtle, take a breath of air and hold it. Others, like the fish, tadpoles, and crayfish, take in oxygen that is dissolved in the water through their gills. The whirligig beetle takes a bubble of air underwater. The lily pads "breathe" through pores located only on the top of their leaves. Why do you think the pores are only on the top of their leaves? How does Jamey breathe under water?

On *pages 12 and 13,* you can see Megan and the frog sharing air. Birds, animals, and plants share air, too.

On *pages 16 and 17* are some things that smell bad to us. The smell of rotting fish attracts houseflies but makes Jamey hold his nose. The skunk protects itself by releasing a strong odor from a gland near its tail when it wants to keep enemies away.

Pages 18 and 19: Humans and dogs smell with their noses. Bees smell with their antennae.

Pages 20 and 21: Crickets make noise by rubbing their wings together. Their "ears" are in their front legs. What other things can Megan hear?

On *pages 26 and 27,* you can see the water evaporating from lakes and oceans. When it cools, it forms droplets that fall to earth as rain or snow.

Pages 28 and 29: In space, there is no air, and meteoroids travel at great speeds. When they reach the Earth's atmosphere, contact with air causes them to burn up, and they are called meteorites when they hit the ground.

On *pages 30 and 31* are things being moved by the wind. How many can you find? Is it helpful for seeds to be blown by the wind?

Remember, air is all around. Imagine *you* can see it.